THE GUARDIANS

TOOTHIANA
part two

A Queen Takes Flight

Atheneum Books for Young Readers • An imprint of Simon & Schuster Children's Publishing Division • 1230 Avenue of the Americas, New York, New York 10020 • This book is a work of fiction. Any references to historical events, real people, or real places are used fictitiously. Other names, characters, places, and events are products of the author's imagination, and any resemblance to actual events or places or persons, living or dead, is entirely coincidental. • Copyright © 2012 by William Joyce • Rise of the Guardians TM & © 2012 DreamWorks Animation, LLC. "Pitch" character design and related elements used with permission. All rights reserved. • All rights reserved, including the right of reproduction in whole or in part in any form. • ATHENEUM BOOKS FOR YOUNG READERS is a registered trademark of Simon & Schuster, Inc. • Atheneum logo is a trademark of Simon & Schuster, Inc. • For information about special discounts for bulk purchases, please contact Simon & Schuster Special Sales at 1-866-506-1949 or business@simonandschuster.com. • The Simon & Schuster Speakers Bureau can bring authors to your live event. For more information or to book an event, contact the Simon & Schuster Speakers Bureau at 1-866-248-3049 or visit our website at www.simonspeakers.com. • Book design by Lauren Rille • The text for this book is set in Adobe Jenson Pro. • The illustrations for this book are rendered in a combination of charcoal, graphite, and digital media. • Manufactured in the United States of America 1012 OFF • 10 9 8 7 6 5 4 3 2 1 • CIP data for this book is available from the Library of Congress. • ISBN 978-1-4424-7292-1

KATHERINE, NIGHTLIGHT, AND THE OTHER Guardians have come to believe that they have forever vanquished their greatest enemy, Pitch, the Nightmare King, in the great battle at the Earth's core. To both celebrate, and make doubly certain, they decide to head for the steepest peaks of the Himalayan Mountains to confer with the Man in the Moon. They enlist the aid of the newest Guardian, E. Aster Bunnymund, who can dig tunnels at lightning speed. He brings the Guardians and their friends onto his Eggomotive where they travel from their tiny village of Santoff Claussen to the Lunar Lamadary—the place closest on Earth to the Moon. Once contacted, the Man in the Moon seems to confirm their theory. Everyone is elated … everyone, that is, except Nightlight. …

A Tear of Mystery

WITH ALL THE HURLY-BURLY and hubbub surrounding this new Golden Age and the city North would build, Katherine found herself lost in the shuffle. The adult Guardians were in a frenzy of excitement, talking heatedly among themselves. She didn't mind, really. It made her happy to see North and Ombric in deep discussions again; it was like old times. And watching Bunnymund interject ideas was always amusing. He was enthusiastic as long as the plans involved chocolate or eggs. As the discussions went on, she realized they'd made a slight breakthrough. Bunnymund was now willing to broaden his interest to other types of candies. "Anything that is sweet has great philosophical and curative powers, and as such, could be key to this new Golden Age!" he pronounced with his usual droll pookery.

The villagers of Santoff Claussen were also happily speculating about new innovations and technologies. The children, especially, were caught up in the commotion. Sascha and the youngest William came up to Katherine. "What do you think this all means?" Sascha asked.

Katherine thought a moment, then answered, "It means that there'll be amazing new things to invent and build and see and do." Sascha's and William's eyes grew bright as they tried to imagine what this future would be like.

As if reading their minds, Katherine added, "Everything will be . . . different."

Before they could ask her to explain, she caught a glimpse of Nightlight up on the highest tower of the Lamadary, and she hurried after him. All his dodging about had her increasingly worried. She could not *feel* his friendship. She could feel nothing from him at all.

The steps to the bell tower were steeper than she'd expected and proved hard to climb. North's compass, which she hadn't taken off since he'd given it to her all those long months ago, was swinging back and forth, thunking against her chest in a most annoying way. But she didn't stop to remove it; she just climbed on.

I hope Nightlight hasn't flown off, she thought, trying to see around a corner as she neared the top steps. She began climbing much more quietly. Through an arched window, she could see him on the other side, perched on the ledge. His back was to her, but she could see that his head hung low, almost to his knees. The light from the diamond point of his staff was dim. And for the first time in days, she could sense his feelings; his feelings were sad. Very sad.

She'd never known Nightlight to be sad! She crept closer still, until she could see that he was holding something. Carefully, carefully, without making a sound, she balanced herself out onto the ledge right next to him. In his hand he held something. She leaned forward even closer. It was a tear. A single tear.

Nightlight suddenly realized she was there. He jumped to his feet with an abruptness that startled her. She teetered for a moment, windmilling her arms for balance.

In a terrible instant, she fell from the ledge.

The Tooth of Destiny

FALLING TO YOUR DEATH is a strange and unsettling sensation. Your mind becomes very sharp. Time seems to slow down. You are able to think an incredible number of thoughts at astonishing speed. These were Katherine's thoughts for the three and a half seconds before she came in contact with the cobblestone courtyard of the Lunar Lamadary:

Oh oh oh oh! Falling! I'm falling!!! FAAALL-LING!!!!! Not good!! Maybe I'm not falling. Please-pleasepleasepleeeeese say I'm not falling. WRONG!!! FALLING!!! Falling FAST!!!! FastFastFastFast . . . Slow

DOWN . . . Can't CAN'T . . . Not good . . . Okay . . . think . . . How do I stop? I DON'T KNOW!!!!! Okay, okay, okay . . . I HATE GRAVITY . . . GRAVITY!!! HATE!!! HATE!!! HATE GRAVITY!!!!! Hairs in my mouth . . . My hair . . . Yuck . . . Spit . . . Okay . . . Hairs out of mouth . . . FALLING!!!! STILL FALLING!!!!! A tear? Why was Nightlight holding a tear? . . . Sad . . . real sad . . . SAD!!! SAD THAT I'M FALLING . . . Where is everybody? . . . There are flying people everywhere in this place. . . . FLYING PEOPLE HELP NOW!!!! RIGHT NOW!!! I'M YOUR FALLING FRIEND HERE . . . FALLING FAAAAAST . . . I MEAN IT!!! Where are all my magic flying friends? . . . Hellooo . . . falling Katherine . . . could USE A HAND . . . NOW!!!! Now NOW NOW NOWWWWWW!!! Is that Nightlight? . . . Can't tell . . . OH NO TURNING FALLING FAST DOWN GROUND COMING NOT GOOD

NOT GOOD NOT GOOD . . . GROUND . . .
Happy thoughts . . . kittens . . . chocolate . . . baby mice . . .
family . . . friends . . . family . . . favorite pillow . . . friends . . .
favorite pillow . . . North . . . Ombric . . . MOON . . . Bun-
nymund . . . North . . . Nightlight . . . NIGHTLIGHT!
NIGHTLIGHT! NIGHTLIGHT! SAVE ME!!!

Then, as she screamed and thought her life was ended, her chin came into contact with the cobblestone courtyard, and she suddenly stopped falling. Nightlight had caught her left foot.

He was floating.

So now Katherine was as well. Or almost. Her chin nicked against a cobblestone, but the rest of her was held aloft. For a moment she was speechless. And when she did try to talk, she found it difficult. There was something small and hard in her mouth, like a pebble. She instinctively spit it onto the ground beneath her. Out bounced not a pebble but . . . a tooth! Her tooth. Her last baby tooth.

And before she could even say "ouch," chimes rang out as every bell in the Lunar Lamadary began to toll. And suddenly the entire troop of Lamas and the Yetis were surrounding her and Nightlight. They were chanting and bowing and bowing and chanting.

"Most auspicious," said the Grand High Lama.

"A tooth . . . ," said another.

". . . of a child . . . ," said a taller one.

". . . of a Guardian child . . . ," said a roundish one.

"A lost tooth . . . ," said the shortest one.

"The TOOTH . . . ," said the Grand High Lama with a touch of awe, ". . . OF DESTINY!"

Then they started up bowing and chanting again. Nightlight gently lowered Katherine to the ground, then helped her up, and together they stood, baffled.

Katherine, Nightlight,
and the bond of the lost tooth

But even more baffling to Katherine was the strange look on Nightlight's face. He was trying to hide it. But he didn't know how. He was so confused by all that was happening and how close he'd come to losing Katherine. She was growing up. Nightlight's worst fear—his *only* fear—was coming true. He did not understand growing up. He did not know if he could grow up. And he did not want to be left behind if she did. But he had saved her, and as she placed her finger in the empty spot where her tooth had been, he knew that everything would be different. But there was only one thing he could do—smile at the gap in her grin.

A Teasing Tale
of Teeth and Terror

I**T TOOK** N**ORTH**, O**MBRIC**, and Bunnymund a few minutes to shift gears from planning a new Golden Age to understanding the importance of Katherine's lost tooth.

They had been gathered in conference in the Lamadary library when the Lunar Lamas filled the chamber, presenting Katherine and her tooth with great pomp and circumstance, proclaiming it "a lost tooth of destiny."

Bunnymund was particularly vexed by the interruption. "If Katherine is unharmed, then what is all this fuss about a tooth?" he asked, one ear twitching. "It isn't actually lost. She holds it in her hand, and now she'll grow another one. It's all very natural and, frankly, rather ordinary. It's not like she lost a chocolate truffled egg or anything."

Then the Grand High Lama described Katherine's fall and hairbreadth rescue.

Bunnymund felt a twinge of shame. He didn't mean to discount Katherine's terrifying accident. But still, a tooth was just a tooth.

The Lamas pressed on.

"We Lamas do not have baby teeth to lose," explained the Grand High Lama.

"At least, not since before recorded time," added the shortest Lama.

"And we've never had a child at the Lamadary...," said the tallest Lama.

"... who's lost a child's tooth," said the least ancient Lama.

"So we've never been visited by Her Most Royal Highness," stressed the Grand High Lama.

The mention of a "Most Royal Highness" piqued everyone else's collective interest.

"Her Most Royal Highness who?" asked North, certain that if this personage dwelled on this continent, he'd likely stolen something from her in his crime-filled younger years. Ombric leaned forward, also eager to hear the Lamas' answer.

The Grand High Lama actually looked shocked by their ignorance. "Why, Her Most Royal Highness, Queen Toothiana, gatherer and protector of children's lost teeth!"

Well, that raised eyebrows from every one of them. Everyone except Bunnymund.

"Oh, her," he said dismissively. "She dislikes chocolate. She claims it's bad for children's teeth." He sniffed. "For confectionery's sake, they all fall out, anyway."

But Ombric, North, and especially Katherine wanted to know more. "I've read something about her once, I believe—" Ombric was saying, trying to remember, when a quiet cough interrupted him.

They all turned. Mr. Qwerty was standing on one of the library's Moon-shaped tables.

"Mr. Qwerty knows something," Katherine said.

The bookworm bowed and told them, "The story of the Queen of Toothiana lies in volume six of *Curious Unexplainables of the East*."

"Of course! I should have remembered that myself," Ombric said, nodding. "Mr. Qwerty, please enlighten us."

The Guardians sat around the table while Mr. Qwerty began his tale.

A Sister of Flight

"To know the story of Queen Toothiana," he said, "you must first hear the tale of the maharaja, his slave Haroom, and the Sisters of Flight."

"Sisters of Flight?" North interrupted.

"Sisters of Flight," Mr. Qwerty repeated patiently. The image of a beautiful winged woman appeared on one of Mr. Qwerty's pages. She was human-size, with long, willowy arms and legs and a heart-shaped face. But her wings were magnificent, and she held a bow and arrow of extraordinary design.

"Can she really fly?" Katherine asked in awe.

"Please, allow me to tell

the tale," Mr. Qwerty said. "The Sisters of Flight were an immortal race of winged women who ruled the city of Punjam Hy Loo, which sits atop the steepest mountain in the mysterious lands of the Farthest East. An army of noble elephants stood guard at the base of the mountain. No humans were allowed to enter, for the mountain's jungle was a haven for the beasts of the wild—a place where they could be safe from men and their foolishness."

Bunnymund's nose twitched. "Men are certainly full of *that*," he agreed.

North's nostrils flared, ready to argue with the Pooka, but Mr. Qwerty quietly continued.

"Toothiana's father was a human by the name of Haroom. He had been sold at birth into slavery as a companion for a young Indian maharaja. Despite being slave and master, the maharaja and Haroom

*Haroom, the slave with
the heart of a prince*

became great friends. But the maharaja was a silly, vain boy who had his every wish and whim granted. Yet this did not make him happy, for he always wanted more.

"Haroom, who had nothing, wanted nothing and so was very content. Secretly, the maharaja admired his friend for this. For his part, Haroom admired the maharaja for knowing what he wanted—and getting it."

Katherine scooted closer to Mr. Qwerty, peeking at the images of Haroom and the maharaja that now appeared on his pages. *How had a slave become the father of a queen?*

Mr. Qwerty straightened his pages and continued. "The maharaja loved to hunt and slay all the animals of the wild, and Haroom, who never tired of watching the powerful elegance of wild creatures such as tigers and snow leopards, was an excellent tracker. But he hated to see the animals killed, so when that moment came, he always looked away. As a slave, he could do nothing to stop his master. And so, with Haroom tracking, the maharaja killed one of every beast in his kingdom, lining the palace walls with their heads as trophies. But the one animal the maharaja coveted most continued to elude him.

"In the mountain land ruled by the Sisters of Flight, there dwelled one creature that no slave, man, or ruler had ever seen: the flying elephant of Punjam Hy Loo."

Katherine was impressed. "A flying *elephant?*"

Mr. Qwerty nodded. "Indeed, a flying elephant. The maharaja was determined to do anything to have one for his collection, but every time he tried to force his way up the mountain, the elephant army at its base turned him back. He realized that he must find another way to reach Punjam Hy Loo.

"In those ancient times no man had yet discovered the mystery of flight. But after demanding advice from his wizards and soothsayers, the maharaja learned a secret: Children can fly when they dream, and when the Moon shines brightly, their dreams can become so vivid that some of them come true. Sometimes the children remember, but mostly they do not. That is why children sometimes wake up in their parents' beds without knowing how they got there—they flew!

"The wizards told the maharaja a second secret." At this, Mr. Qwerty lowered his voice, and all the Guardians leaned closer. "The memory of everything that happens to a child is stored in that child's baby teeth.

"And so the maharaja's wizards gave him an idea: fashion a craft of the lost teeth of children and command it to remember how to fly. The maharaja sent out a decree throughout his kingdom, stating that whenever a child lost a tooth, it must be brought to his palace. His subjects happily complied, and it was not long before he had assembled a craft unlike any other the world had ever known."

Once again an image formed on one of Mr. Qwerty's blank pages. It was of a ship of gleaming white, fashioned from thousands of interlocking teeth. It had wings on each side of an oval gondola. The inside was lined with sumptuous carpets and intricately patterned pillows. And a single lamp hung from a mast to light the way.

"Meanwhile, the maharaja ordered Haroom to make an archer's bow of purest gold and one single ruby-tipped arrow. When the weapon was finished, the maharaja ordered Haroom to join him aboard the craft. Then he said these magic words:

> *"Remember,*
> *remember,*
> *the moonlit flights*
> *of magic nights."*

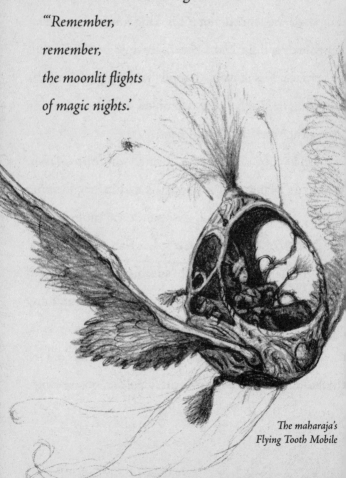

The maharaja's
Flying Tooth Mobile

"And just as the royal wizards had promised, the craft flew silently through the sky, over the jungle, and past the elephants who guarded Punjam Hy Loo.

"They descended from the clouds and flew into the still-sleeping city. In the misty light of dawn, the maharaja could hardly tell where the jungle ended and the city began. But Haroom, used to seeking out tracks, spotted some he had never seen before— tracks that could only belong to the flying elephant, for although they looked similar to a normal elephant's, his keen eye saw one addition: an extra digit pointing backward, like that of a bird.

"It did not take long to find the flying elephant, sleeping in a nest in the low-lying limbs of an enormous jujube tree. The maharaja raised the golden bow and took careful aim. The tip of the ruby arrow glittered in the first rays of morning sunlight. Haroom looked away.

"Suddenly, there came an intense, cacophonous alarm, as if every creature of Punjam Hy Loo knew of the maharaja's murderous intent. Charging down from the towers above came the Sisters of Flight, wings outstretched, with all manner of weapons at the ready—gleaming

The flying elephant of Punjam Hy Loo

swords, razor-sharp daggers, fantastical flying spears with wings of their own. It was a sight so beautiful, so terrifying that Haroom and the maharaja froze.

"Then the maharaja raised his bow again, this time aiming it at the Sisters of Flight. 'Look, Haroom, an even greater prize,' he exclaimed.

"In that single moment Haroom's whole life changed. He knew, for the very first time, what he wanted. He could not bear to see a Sister of Flight harmed. He ordered the maharaja to stop.

"The maharaja paid his servant no heed. He let loose the arrow. Haroom blocked it. Its ruby tip pierced his chest, and he crumbled to the ground.

"The maharaja stared in shock, then kneeled beside his fallen friend. Weeping, he tried to stop the flow of blood but could not. Haroom was dying.

The Sisters of Flight landed around them. The

most beautiful of the sisters, the one the maharaja had meant to kill, approached them. 'We did not know that any man could be so selfless,' she said. Her sisters nodded.

"With one hand, she grabbed the arrow and plucked it from Haroom's chest, then kissed her fingertips and gently touched his wound.

"Haroom stirred, and his eyes fluttered open. All he could see was the face of the Sister of Flight. And all she could see was the brave and noble Haroom.

"He was a slave no more.

"She took his hand, and in that instant her wings vanished.

"The other sisters lunged toward the maharaja in fury. They raised their swords, and Haroom could see they meant to kill his former master. 'He will no longer harm you,' he said. 'Please, let him go—send him on his way.'

"The sisters looked from one to the other, then agreed. But they declared that the maharaja must leave all he brought with him. The golden bow, the ruby-tipped arrow, the flying craft of teeth, and Haroom, his only friend.

"'And one thing more.

"'You must also leave your vanity and cruelty behind so that we can know and understand them.'

"The maharaja was heartbroken but agreed.

"The flying elephant glided down from his nest, and with his trunk, he touched the maharaja's forehead, and all the vanity and cruelty went from him.

"But once these things were gone, there was little left—the maharaja was as simple as a baby monkey. In fact, he even sprouted a tail and scampered away speaking gibberish, shrinking to the size of an infant.

"His vanity and cruelty would never be forgotten—the flying elephant had them now, and an elephant never forgets. As for Haroom and the beautiful Sister of Flight, they were married and lived on in Punjam Hy Loo. Within a year, a child was born. A girl. Selfless like her father. Pure of heart like her mother. She was named Toothiana."

Toothiana as a child

The Story of Queen Toothiana Continues:
A Mystery of Wing and Madness

MR. QWERTY TOOK A sip of tea and continued: "The child of Haroom and Rashmi (for that was Toothiana's mother's name) seemed to be a normal mortal child. As there were no other human children living in Punjam Hy Loo, her parents thought it best to raise her among other mortals, and so they settled on the outskirts of a small village at the edge of the jungle. The young girl was well loved and protected and lived a simple, happy life until she was twelve and lost her last baby tooth. That's when all her troubles began."

"Troubles?" Katherine asked nervously.

"Yes, troubles," Mr. Qwerty said. "For when she lost her last baby tooth, Toothiana sprouted wings. By the end of this first miraculous day, she could fly with the speed of a bird, darting to the top of the tallest trees to choose the ripest mangoes, papayas, and starfruit for the children of the village. She played with the birds and made friends with the wind.

"But while the children delighted in Toothiana's new skill, the adults of the village were bewildered, even frightened, by this half bird, half girl. Some thought she was an evil spirit and should be killed; others saw ways to use her, as either a freak to be caged and paraded about, or to force her to fly to the palace of the new maharaja and steal his jewels.

"Haroom and Rashmi knew that to keep their daughter safe, they would have to pack their few belongings and escape. And so they did, deep into the jungle. The village children, all of whom adored Toothiana, tried to persuade their parents to leave her alone. But it was no use. The grown-ups of the village had gone mad with fear and greed.

"They built a large cage, hired the best hunters in the land, and asked them to capture the young girl. Among these was a hunter most mysterious. He spoke not a word and was shrouded from head to foot in tattered cloth stitched together with jungle vines. The villagers were wary of him, and even the other hunters found him peculiar. 'He knows the jungle better than any of us—it's as if he's more a creature than a man,' they remarked quietly among themselves.

"But Haroom and Rashmi were as wily as any hunter. Haroom, knowing everything there was to know about tracking, could disguise their trail so that no one could follow it. And Rashmi, who could converse with any animal, enlisted their aid in confounding the hunters. Tigers, elephants, even giant pythons would intercept the hunters whenever they neared. But the hunters, eager for the riches and fame they'd receive if they caged Toothiana, would not give up."

Why can grown-ups be so strange and wicked sometimes? Katherine wondered, not asking aloud so as not to stop Mr. Qwerty's story. He cleared his throat and continued.

"The children of the village were also determined to thwart the hunters. They defied their parents, sending word to Toothiana and her mother and father again and again whenever the hunters were stalking the jungle. Toothiana, wiser still, hid in the treetops by day, only visiting her parents in the darkest hours of the night.

"After weeks of the best hunters in the land failing to capture Toothiana, the cunning villagers became more sly. They secretly followed their children and discovered where Toothiana's parents were hiding. They left a trail of coins for the hunters to follow. But only one hunter came—the one they almost feared. It was then that the Mysterious Hunter finally spoke. His voice was strange, high-pitched, almost comical, but his words were cold as death. 'Seize the parents,' he snarled. 'Make it known that I will slit their throats if Toothiana does not surrender. That will bring this child of flight out of hiding.'

"His plan made sense; the villagers did as he suggested. They attacked Haroom and Rashmi's camp.

With so many against them, the two surrendered without a fight. They had told their clever daughter to never try and help them if they were ever captured.

"But the Mysterious Hunter had planned for that. He shouted out to any creature that could hear, 'The parents of the flying girl will die by dawn if she comes not!'

"The creatures of the jungle hurried to warn Toothiana that her parents were doomed if she did not come. Toothiana had never disobeyed her parents, but the thought of them at the dubious mercy of these grown-ups filled her with rage and determination, and she flew straight to her parents' aid. She dove down from the treetops, ready to kill any who would try to harm her parents.

"But Haroom and Rashmi were brave and cunning as well. Haroom, who had never harmed a living creature, was prepared to stop at nothing to prevent his daughter from being enslaved. And Rashmi, like all Sisters of Flight, had been a great warrior. As Toothiana neared, they slashed and fought like beings possessed. Toothiana flickered back and forth, hovering over her mother and father, reaching for them, but she did not have the strength to lift them up over the angry mob. Rashmi thrust a stringed pouch into her daughter's hands. 'Keep these to remember us by. Keep these to protect yourself,' she pleaded to her child.

"'Now go!' commanded her father. 'GO!'

"With a heartrending cry, the winged girl did as her father ordered. She flew away but stopped, unsure of what to do. Her ears filled with the sound of the vengeful mob falling upon her parents.

"'Go!' shouted her mother.

"Toothiana flew wildly and desperately away. And as she went, she screamed from the depths of her soul. It was the scream of two beings: human and animal. It was a scream so pained and fierce that it caused all the villagers who were attacking her parents to go briefly deaf. All except . . . the Mysterious Hunter. He screamed back to Toothiana. His was a scream equally unsettling—a scream of rage and hate that was more animal than human. Toothiana knew in that instant that she had a mortal enemy—one who she must kill or be killed by.

"But for now she would grieve. She flew to the highest treetop and huddled deep inside its foliage. She had no tears, only the blank ache of a now-empty life. She rocked back and forth in a trance of disbelief for a full day and night. Then she remembered the pouch her mother had thrust into her hands. Trembling, she opened it. Inside was a small box carved from a single giant ruby. It was covered in feathery patterns, and Toothiana knew that the box had once been the ruby-tipped arrow that had nearly killed her parents. Inside this beautiful box was a cluster of baby teeth and a note: —

Our Dearest Girl,

These are the teeth of your childhood. If you have them under your pillow as you sleep, or hold it tightly, you will remember that which you need — a memory of happy days, or of deepest hopes, or even of us in better times.

But one tooth is not yours. It is a tooth of amazing power, and from what being it comes from, we do not know.

*Use it only in times of the greatest
danger or need.
Your Dearest Parents*

"Toothiana still did not cry, not even after reading the note. She slept with her baby teeth under her pillow and took solace in the dreams and memories it gave her."

Lost Teeth and a Purpose Found

Toothiana stayed in the jungle. She began to hate her wings. Once, she had thought them wondrous things, but now she saw them as the reason for the death of her parents. Her grief and loneliness knew no depths. The creatures of the jungle did what they could to help her, by bringing her food and making her treetop sleeping places as comfortable as possible. The children of the village tried to aid as well, but they now had to be doubly cautious of the village grown-ups.

"As for Toothiana, she became more and more

convinced that she belonged nowhere—not among the creatures of the jungle and certainly not among the humans of the village. She was alone. When she was at her very saddest, she would take one of her baby teeth from the carved box she always carried in her mother's pouch she now wore around her neck, and hold it until it revealed its memories.

"As the lonely years passed, Toothiana saw that the village children lost much of their innocence and some of their goodness as they grew up. She began to collect their teeth, so that, in the future, she could give them back their childhood memories and remind them of their kindness, just as her own parents had done for her.

"Soon the children, not wanting their parents to find out, began to hide their lost teeth under their pillows for Toothiana to find. And she, cheered by this new game of sorts, began in turn to leave behind small bits of treasure she had found in the jungle. A gold nugget here. A sprinkling of sapphire chips there.

"But you can imagine the curiosity that is stirred when a five-year-old sits down to breakfast with an uncut ruby in her palm, or when a ten-year-old boy comes to the table with a pocket full of emeralds. Once again the hearts of the grown-ups filled with greed, and it wasn't long before they forced their children to tell them how they had come upon those treasures. Soon enough they had laid a new trap for Toothiana.

"One dark, cloudy night Toothiana flew to the village to make her nightly rounds. A boy named Akela had lost his two front teeth, and Toothiana had a special treasure saved for him: two beautiful uncut diamonds. But as she entered his open window, it wasn't Akela she found. Instead the Mysterious Hunter leaped toward her. From behind his shroud of rags, she could see the strangest eyes. Close together. Beady. Not entirely human. And cold with hate.

"Toothiana's rage clouded her keen intellect. All she could think was, *I must get rid of this . . . thing!* But before she could act, a steel door slammed down between her and the Hunter. She glanced around with birdlike quickness. The room was not Akela's bedroom, but, in fact, a cleverly disguised steel cage.

"She was trapped! The villagers cheered as the Hunter hauled away the cage. His platoon of slave-like helpers pulled the wheeled prison away from the villagers and into the jungle. The helpers were as strangely shrouded as the Hunter who commanded them was, and seemed excited by the capture. The children wept, begging their parents to let Toothiana go free. But they would not. The Mysterious Hunter had promised them riches beyond their dreams when he sold Toothiana.

"Toothiana flung herself wildly against the cage, like a cornered eagle. But it did no good. The Hunter and his minions traveled swiftly through the night, deeper into the jungle. They knew the creatures of the wild would try to help Toothiana, so they carried the one weapon every animal fears: fire.

"Torches were lashed to the roof of Toothiana's cage. The Mysterious Hunter himself carried the brightest torch of all. The animals kept their distance, but they continued to follow the eerie caravan and keep watch over Toothiana, waiting for a chance to strike.

"After days of travel they arrived at the base of the steep mountain of Toothiana's birthplace—the kingdom of Punjam Hy Loo. The great elephants that guarded the mountain were standing at the ready, shifting back and forth on their massive feet. Toothiana's jungle friends had warned them that the Mysterious Hunter was headed their way.

"The Hunter did not challenge the elephants. He ordered his minions to halt and made no move to attack. Instead, he held his flaming torch aloft. 'I bring a treasure to the Sisters of Flight and the flying elephant king who dwell in Punjam Hy Loo!' he shouted into the night sky. The sky was empty; there was no sign of either the winged women who ruled there, or of the flying elephant.

"The Hunter called out again. 'I bring you the half-breed daughter of Haroom and Rashmi.' At this, an otherworldly sound—like a rustle of trees in the wind—was heard. And indeed wind did begin to blow down from the mountain. It grew stronger and more furious, with gusts that nearly put out the torches.

"Toothiana knew instinctually that this wind was sent by the Sisters of Flight and that they did not trust the Hunter. She also knew that it was time to take out the box her parents had left her.

"As the winds continued to rise, the Hunter grew increasingly nervous, as did his minions. They began to chatter in the oddest way, not in words, but in sounds.

"Then a chorus of voices, all speaking in unison, rang out bright and clear above the howl of the wind: 'Tell us, Hunter, why cage our child? Where be her father and mother? What trick of men do you bring us? What do you seek, you who seem of men and yet are not?'

"The Hunter rocked on his feet, seething with undisguised hate. He held his torch high and stepped forward, leaning into the wind. The elephants raised their trunks but took a step back. Fire was a fearsome thing, even for these mighty beasts.

"The Hunter laughed, then threw down his tattered cloak. He was no man at all, but a massive monkey. 'A maharaja of men I once was,' he screamed, 'and by your doing, I am now a king of the monkeys!' Then his troops dropped their cloaks as well. An array of monkeys revealed themselves, all armed with bows and arrows.

"The Monkey King shrieked above the roaring wind, 'You ask about her parents? Dead! By *my* doing! What do I seek? Revenge! On all who made me thus!' Then he threw his torch into the herd of elephants and grabbed a bow and arrow from one of his men. He had it drawn in an instant, aimed directly at Toothiana's heart.

"Before he could let loose the arrow, the wind tripled in strength. Toothiana knew what to do. She held the ruby box tightly in her hand. 'Mother, Father, help me,' she whispered furiously, clenching her eyes shut. She pictured them clearly in her mind, letting herself feel the bond they had shared so deeply, letting herself remember how much they had sacrificed for her.

"Suddenly, she was no longer in the cage. She was no longer a single entity, but several smaller versions of herself.

"Bow drawn, the Monkey King hesitated, bewildered. *How can this be?* He could not remember the power of love—even though it had been this girl's father who had loved him best—and his own memories were now fueled only by hate.

"So the world turned against him once again.

"The Sisters of Flight circled overhead. It was the flapping of their wings that made the great wind. It grew wilder and stranger, like a tornado. Leaves snapped off trees. Dirt swirled like a storm, and the Monkey King's torch blew out.

"Now the only light came from the Moon, and no jungle creature fears that guiding light. In an instant the elephants stampeded forward. Toothiana's animal friends attacked. Toothiana's mini-selves charged the Monkey King. The monkey army screamed and ran.

"The king tried to grab the Toothianas, but he could not catch them. Then all the fairy-sized selves merged back into a single being.

A mini Tooth

Toothiana was mystified by her new power, but she didn't think on it. With one hand, she grabbed the Monkey King by the throat. It was as if she now had the strength of a dozen. The Monkey King cried out in terror and pain.

"For an instant Toothiana felt the rage within her swell. She would snap his neck and be done with him. But the little box glowed in one hand, and the memory of her parents made her stop. She would not end this monkey man's life. Let the jungle choose his fate.

"So she let him go.

"He fell to the ground, and she did not look back as she flew up to join the Sisters of Flight.

"As they sped away, Toothiana and her kindred could hear the creatures of the jungle do as they saw fit with the fallen Monkey King. And his cries could be heard all the way to the Moon."

Mr. Qwerty then shut his pages. The tale, as it was written, was done.

Toothiana's story made Katherine feel many things, but the strangest was a twinge of envy. *Toothiana* had memories of *her* parents. It was something Katherine wished for more than anything.

Nightlight Faces
the Unknown

AFTER LISTENING AT THE window to the story of Queen Toothiana, Nightlight flew listlessly around the mountains that surrounded the Lunar Lamadary. He was increasingly troubled. Until now he had viewed the events of his life in very simple terms. To him, the world was divided into good and bad. Katherine and the Guardians were good—absolutely. And Pitch was bad, through and through, without even an ounce of good in him. And yet . . .

Nightlight was confounded by what he had seen in Katherine's Dream Tear. And in this dream, Pitch's hand was human, as it had been since he'd tried to make Nightlight a Darkling Prince.

But there was more.

In the dream, Pitch had held in his human hand the locket with his daughter's picture. But the picture shifted, and Katherine's face took its place. And then *her* face began to change! It became different. Older. A grown-up's face. And then darker. More like Pitch's.

Nightlight was afraid of this dream. It felt true. No Guardian had seen any sign of Pitch of late, yet Nightlight had; Pitch *lived*—in Katherine's dreams. What did this mean?

Would she grow up? Would she become like so many adults, a grim shadow of her youthful self? Or was there a greater danger? Would she somehow be taken over by Pitch? Was her soul in danger? These questions tore at his heart and soul in ways he could not comprehend or put into words. So he turned to his oldest friend.

For hours he waited for the Moon to rise, and when it did, he took Katherine's Dream Tear and held it up. The moonbeam inside his staff began to flash, and moments later, the Man in the Moon responded to his signal. Moonbeams shined down and flickered as they interpreted the Dream Tear. Then Nightlight, waiting anxiously, finally whispered in his rarely used and otherworldly voice, "Will my Katherine go Darkling or stay true?" He stood, still and tense, for a long while until a moonbeam brought back the simple answer, the answer that was the truth of everything:

Believe. Believe. Believe, it said.

And for the first time in his endless childhood life, Nightlight cried. He was not sure why he was crying.

He could not describe the feeling that brought the tears. It was not happiness or sorrow. It was not good or bad. But it was something just as powerful.

Someday he would know what it was, that first mysterious step beyond childhood. It is a strange feeling, to realize that you will grow up, especially for one who has been a child for so long. But he now had the answer he needed to face this uncertainty.

Believe. Believe. Believe. If he could remember that, he would make everything right. And so his tears stopped. He wiped them from his cheeks, then brought them close to his face, so unaccustomed was he to having tears.

Each was bright with light and seemed to take the burden from his anxious heart. He let them spill together with Katherine's Dream Tear.

Then he took the diamond tip of his staff and

touched it to the tears, holding it there until they fused with the diamond. Now the spearlike point of his staff held not just his friend's fear and sorrow, but his own as well.

The moonbeam inside grew furiously bright, for sorrow and fear that are triumphed over make a powerful weapon.

At that instant he heard Katherine calling for him, and he knew that whatever might come, he was ready.

Plots, Plans, and Pillows

I**T IS NOT EASY** to fall asleep when an entire village, an army of Abominable Snowmen, a troupe of ancient Lunar holy men, and all your best friends are coming into your bedroom and wishing you good night. It is also not easy to sleep when you know you are going to be visited by a half-bird, half-human queen with magical powers. And it is really hard to sleep when you have made a secret plan with your dearest friend to do the *one thing* you've been told you absolutely MUST NOT DO when this particular queen arrives. So there Katherine sat, in her huge and feathered bed in her special room in the Lunar Lamadary, as wide awake as any twelve-year-old has ever been.

She'd just checked under her pillow for the eleventh time to make certain that her tooth hadn't somehow rolled onto the floor when North opened the bedroom door again, just enough to stick in his head. "Still awake?" he asked in surprise.

Ombric and Bunnymund crowded in next to him, crammed so tightly in the doorway that Katherine could see only half of Ombric's face and one of Bunnymund's ears, with Ombric's beard tangled around it.

"Perhaps if you chant the ancient Atlantan phrase 'Sleep-o deep-o slumberly doo—'" Ombric began to suggest.

Bunnymund interrupted with, "Counting! That'll do it. Count chocolate eggs jumping counterclockwise over a small wall also made of chocolate—"

Then North interrupted, saying, "A song! We should sing a song!"

Then they all began to talk at once: "It should be about eggs! A sleepy chocolate egg opera would be perfect!" . . . "No, no, no! A good old-fashioned Cossack lullaby. 'Don't cut my throat while I am sleeping, mother, my mother dear.'" . . . "North, that's awful! No, she should chant, 'Dream, dream, dream of chocolate ocean waves . . .'"

And so it went till Nightlight flew down from the rafters and, with a firm but caring swing of his staff, slammed the door shut.

The three Guardians muttered outside the door for a moment or two, then the Lunar Lamas could be heard suggesting that the centuries-old method of simply being left quietly alone tended to bring about sleep quite reliably. And so things finally settled down.

Nightlight leaped to Katherine's bed and sat cross-legged on the footboard. He still seemed . . . different to her; no longer quite so sad or distant. But the cheerful half grin that had always been there was replaced by a look that seemed—well, she couldn't really put a finger on it, but he didn't seem quite so like a little boy now.

And whether it was the Lamas' suggestion or just the result of a very full day, Katherine suddenly felt overcome with sleepiness and ready to close her eyes. But she propped herself up on one elbow for another minute, careful not to shift the pillow that covered her tooth. She wanted to go over the plan she'd concocted earlier with Nightlight one more time. It had come to her when the Lunar Lamas had told her even more details about the workings of Queen Toothiana. It had taken a while, given the Lamas' propensity for vague answers, but Katherine had learned that she had to be asleep for Toothiana to come and take her tooth. And only Toothiana could unlock the countless memories in a tooth, by holding it in her magic grasp. Once the memories were unlocked, Katherine wanted her tooth back.

"You must get my tooth back the instant she does her magic!" she reminded Nightlight.

Nightlight nodded. He could feel how much this meant to Katherine. *She wants to remember her mother and father*, thought Nightlight. *And if she remembers them, then perhaps she'll forget Pitch.*

That's what he believed in his hopeful heart. He had never failed Katherine before, and he would not fail her now.

TO BE CONTINUED . . .

Katherine can scarcely sleep. She's just lost her very last baby tooth, and she's just found out that within every baby tooth are all of the memories of the child who lost it. Now she wants nothing more than to ask Queen Toothiana, who only visits when a tooth is lost, to tell her the memories locked inside the tooth she has under her pillow, for she is sure that then she might finally remember something about her parents.

With her best friend, Nightlight, Katherine carefully strategizes a way to ensure that she'll wake up upon Toothiana's arrival. But meeting the queen doesn't go at all the way the two friends have so carefully planned ... for the queen is used to children trying to spy her, and knows how to thwart this. But what the queen *doesn't* know is that something else is spying on her—something of the simian kind. What they want is as precious to her as Katherine's tooth is to Katherine, and whom they want it for is the Guardian's greatest nightmare.

———◆———

Find out in the next installment of

TOOTHIANA
Panic Sets In